NEW YORK

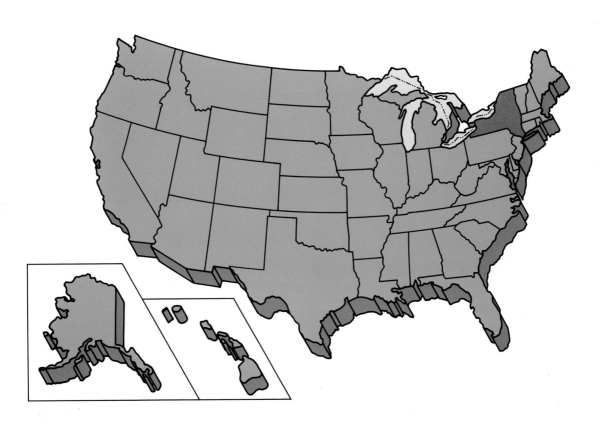

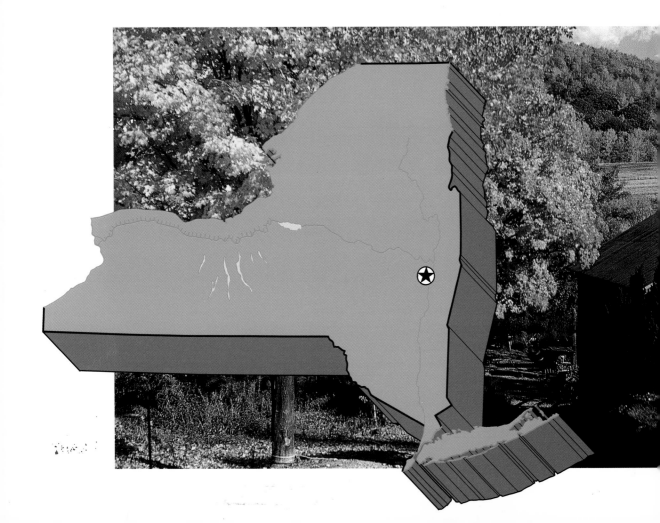

NEW YORK

Amy Gelman

Lerner Publications Company

This book is available in two editions:
Library binding by Lerner Publications Company
Soft cover by First Avenue Editions, 1995
241 First Avenue North
Minneapolis, MN 55401
ISBN: 0-8225-2720-0 (lib. bdg.)
ISBN: 0-8225-9702-0 (pbk.)

LIBRARY OF CONGRESS
CATALOGING-IN-PUBLICATION DATA
Gelman, Amy.
    New York / Amy Gelman.
        p.   cm. — (Hello USA)
    Includes index.
    Summary: An introduction to the state's
geography, history, population, jobs, and en-
vironmental concerns.
        ISBN 0-8225-2720-0 (lib. bdg.)
    1. New York (State)—Juvenile literature.
    [1. New York (State)] I. Title. II. Series.
    F119.3.G45   1992
    974.7—dc20   91-38391

Manufactured in the United States of America
3   4   5   6   -   I/JR   -   99   98   97   96

Cover photograph courtesy of
Bonnie J. Fisher.

The glossary that begins on
page 68 gives definitions of
words shown in **bold type** in
the text.

 This book is printed
on acid-free, recycla-
ble paper.

CONTENTS

Did You Know . . . ?

☐ Hot dogs were first sold, under the name "dachshund sausages," on Coney Island in Brooklyn, New York, in 1871. In 1901 cartoonist Thomas A. Dorgan drew a cartoon of barking dachshund sausages. Since he couldn't spell "dachshund," Dorgan called them "hot dogs," and the name stuck.

☐ New York City has the longest subway system in the country. If all the subway tracks in New York City were laid end to end, they would stretch all the way to Detroit, Michigan—a distance of 637 miles (1025 kilometers).

☐ The Dutch people who settled in New York in the 1600s left their mark on the English language. Some familiar English words that come from Dutch include *cookie, yacht,* and *boss.*

New York City was the first capital of the United States. The nation's first congress held its meetings in New York City from 1785 to 1790.

Amelia Bloomer lived in Seneca Falls, New York, in the mid-1800s. At that time, American women didn't have the same rights as men. But Bloomer believed that women should be allowed to do everything men could do—including wearing pants. The baggy pants she wore were called "bloomers" in her honor, and that's what they've been called ever since.

New York boasts the nation's biggest city, New York City, but it also offers plenty of quiet countryside.

A Trip Around the State

Many people think only of New York City when they think of New York. They imagine skyscrapers, bright lights, crowds of people. But the state of New York boasts much more than just its most famous city. Stretching from the Atlantic Ocean to Lake Erie, from the beaches of Long Island to the peaks of the Appalachian Mountains, New York's landscape is varied and lively.

New York borders five northeastern states —Vermont, Massachusetts, Connecticut, New Jersey, and Pennsylvania. Canada lies to the north, and Lakes Ontario and Erie, two of the **Great Lakes,** cross New York's northern and western boundaries.

Thousands of years ago, glaciers changed the shape of the Adirondack Mountains, in northern New York.

The landscape owes much of its appearance to **glaciers,** vast blocks of ice that covered the region tens of thousands of years ago. As the glaciers melted, they left their mark on almost everything in their path.

They ground their way over ancient mountains such as the Adirondacks, changing their size and shape. The glaciers also carved out hollows in the earth that filled with water to form thousands of lakes around the state.

Over time, glaciers and other natural forces created four types of land in New York—upland, lowland, plateau, and coastal plain.

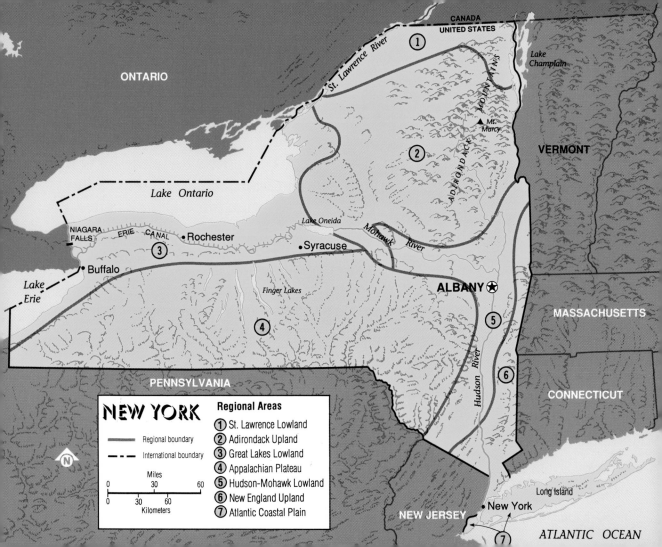

CANADA
UNITED STATES

ONTARIO

VERMONT

Mt. Marcy

Lake Champlain

St. Lawrence River

① St. Lawrence Lowland

② Adirondack Upland

ADIRONDACK MOUNTAINS

Lake Ontario

Lake Oneida

Mohawk River

NIAGARA FALLS

ERIE CANAL

③

• Rochester

• Syracuse

ALBANY ✪

MASSACHUSETTS

• Buffalo

Lake Erie

Finger Lakes

⑤

⑥

Hudson River

CONNECTICUT

④

PENNSYLVANIA

NEW YORK

Regional boundary

International boundary

Miles
0   30   60

0   30   60
Kilometers

N

Regional Areas

① St. Lawrence Lowland
② Adirondack Upland
③ Great Lakes Lowland
④ Appalachian Plateau
⑤ Hudson-Mohawk Lowland
⑥ New England Upland
⑦ Atlantic Coastal Plain

Long Island

NEW JERSEY   • New York

⑦

ATLANTIC OCEAN

New York's two upland regions, called the New England Upland and the Adirondack Upland, are in the eastern part of the state. Both regions are hilly and thickly forested. New York's highest peak, Mount Marcy, rises high above the Adirondack Upland.

New York's lowlands are well suited to farming. The Hudson-Mohawk Lowland is a narrow stretch of rich farmland in the southeastern and east central parts of the state. The rolling St. Lawrence Lowland and the wide, flat Great Lakes Lowland, both in northern New York, also have fertile soil.

The Appalachian Plateau, a flat, rocky region famous for its snowy winters, covers much of the southern part of the state. The region consists mostly of small towns and has few cities. Its scenery includes the Finger Lakes (a popular vacation area) and many dairy farms.

In southeastern New York lies the Atlantic Coastal Plain. This low, flat region is known for its beautiful ocean beaches and includes three of New York City's five **boroughs** (counties)—Queens, Brooklyn, and Staten Island.

12

Farms are a common sight in New York's lowland regions.

13

Ausable Lake in the Adirondack
Mountains is one of thousands of
lakes in the state.

Of New York's many rivers, perhaps the best known are the Hudson and the Mohawk, in the eastern part of the state, and the St. Lawrence, on the border between New York and Canada. Long before people had cars or trains, they used these rivers for trade and travel.

New Yorkers enjoy about 8,000 lakes. The largest lake that is entirely within the state's borders is Lake Oneida, near Syracuse.

14

Snowy winters are common in most of New York, including the Hudson River valley.

Some parts of New York have a mild climate and moderate amounts of **precipitation** (rain or other moisture) all year round. But people in northern New York endure long winters with below-freezing temperatures. Huge amounts of snow —often more than 100 inches (254 centimeters) in a season—fall on western New York in winter.

In the New York City area, summers are often hot and humid, with temperatures climbing to 95° F (35° C) or higher. Farther inland, summers

These red fox cubs are among the many mammals found in New York's countryside.

The bluebird is New York's state bird.

are cooler, and by August, evenings can become chilly.

The varying landscapes in New York are home to lots of different animals. Beavers, opossums, and chipmunks scurry around the state's countryside. Larger animals such as red foxes and white-tailed deer live there too.

Crabs, lobsters, whales, sharks, and bluefish are some of the creatures that swim in New York's coastal waters. Many birds, including egrets and terns, wade in the marshes near the state's seashore.

New York's state flower, the rose, grows wild in some areas, and so do black-eyed Susans and Indian pipes, among many other plants. More than 60 percent of New York is covered with forest, and about 150 types of trees, including sugar maples, beeches, oaks, balsam firs, pines, and spruces, grow there.

Black-eyed Susans grow wild in New York.

New York's Story

People probably first settled in the area that is now New York about 10,000 years ago, after the glaciers that once covered the area had melted. Scientists have found pieces of tools and weapons that these people used, and mounds of earth where they buried their dead. But no one knows very much about them. Their descendants are the people we call Native Americans, or Indians.

The first people to live in the New York area probably used tools like these.

18

By the time the first people from Europe came to the area, in the 1500s, two main groups of Indians lived there. The people of one of the groups spoke Algonquian languages, and most of them farmed and hunted near the Hudson and St. Lawrence rivers. These people included the Mahican, the Montauk, the Wappinger, and the Delaware.

The other group, the Iroquois, lived farther west. The Iroquois also farmed, growing crops such as corn and tobacco. Warfare was important to the Iroquois and served as a way for young men to prove they were strong and powerful.

These Mohawk Indians are making a birchbark canoe in one of their villages during the 1700s.

An early European settler drew his impression of an Iroquois warrior.

20

During the 1400s, five Iroquois nations formed a group known as the Iroquois Confederacy. The members of the Confederacy were the Mohawk, the Seneca, the Oneida, the Cayuga, and the Onondaga. They agreed to keep peace among themselves and to protect each other from enemies.

In 1524 Giovanni da Verrazano, an Italian explorer, sailed into the harbor at what is now New York City. Verrazano returned to Europe, but other Europeans followed in the next century. Some of them stayed and changed the lives of New York's Indians forever.

In 1608 Samuel de Champlain, a Frenchman, set up a fur-trading post in Quebec, Canada, not far from what is now northern New York. There he traded with Algonquian tribes from the region. Champlain exchanged European goods for the pelts of beavers, minks, and other furry animals that thrived throughout the area.

In turn, the Algonquian tribes traded some of the French goods with the Iroquois Confederacy, especially with the Mohawk. The Iroquois also took goods by force from the Algonquian tribes who traded with Champlain.

The mighty Hudson River is named for Henry Hudson, a British explorer.

In 1609 an Englishman named Henry Hudson, working for the Dutch government, sailed up the long river that now bears his name. Like many explorers at the time, he was looking for a new way to get from Europe to Asia. Hudson quickly realized that he had not found a passageway to Asia. He liked the territory, though, and found that the Mahican who lived there were willing to trade with Europeans.

Hudson claimed the area for the Dutch, who called it New Netherland. Soon, some Dutch businessmen decided to send Dutch citizens to establish a settlement, or **colony,** in the region. By settling on the land, the Dutch would strengthen their claim to owning it. Thirty Dutch families established a colony at Fort Orange (now Albany) in 1624.

The Dutch colonists were joined by people from the British-run

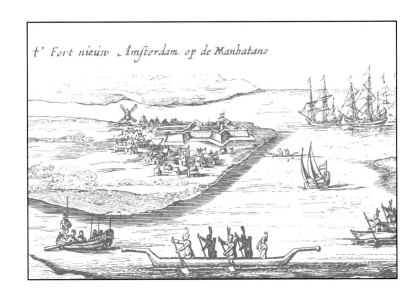

In 1625 the Dutch established a settlement called New Amsterdam at the mouth of the Hudson River.

colonies of Connecticut and Massachusetts Bay. Those colonies did not let everyone practice religion freely, so many people left. People from all over Europe also settled in New Netherland.

In addition, the Dutch took black people from Africa to the colony to be slaves. So although the colony was controlled by the Dutch government, not all of its people were Dutch. People of many different religions, nationalities, and races lived there.

Peter Stuyvesant was the governor of New Netherland from 1647 to 1664.

control New Amsterdam (later New York City), which was an important trading port. In 1664 he sent four British warships into New Amsterdam harbor and gave his brother James a charter claiming the territory.

Peter Stuyvesant, New Netherland's governor, realized the colonists could not defeat the British forces. The Dutch gave up their claim to New Netherland without a fight, and British settlers promptly renamed it New York, after James, Duke of York.

Both the French and the British wanted to profit from the furs they

In 1663 King Charles II of Britain decided to take over the colony of New Netherland. He wanted to

bought from the Indians. Throughout the 1700s, Britain and France fought a series of wars, often called the French and Indian wars. Each country hoped to gain complete control of the territory and its fur trade. Because many important trading posts were located in what is now New York, several battles in the French and Indian wars were fought there.

Most Indians fought on one side or the other in the wars, usually siding with their European trading partners. Many of the Indians who lived in New York fought each other as well. By this time, the five original Iroquois nations had added the Tuscarora, originally from North Carolina, to the league.

Joseph Brant, or Thayendanegea, led his fellow Iroquois in support of the French during the French and Indian wars.

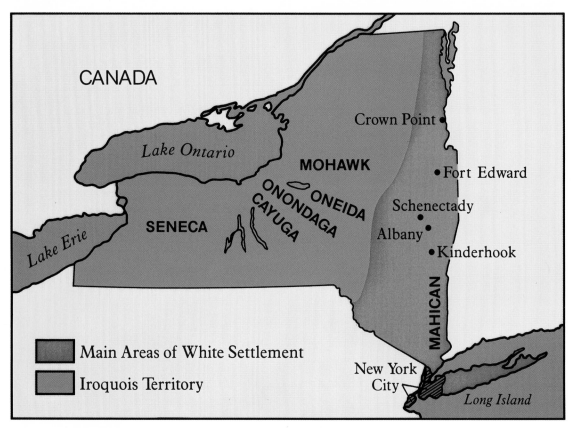

CANADA

Lake Ontario

MOHAWK

Crown Point •

• Fort Edward

ONEIDA

ONONDAGA

CAYUGA

Schenectady
•

Albany •

Lake Erie

SENECA

• Kinderhook

MAHICAN

Main Areas of White Settlement

Iroquois Territory

New York
City

Long Island

In the mid-1700s, most Europeans still lived in the eastern part of what is now New York. The Iroquois controlled the western part of the region. This map shows some of the main cities in the colony of New York and the major tribes in the region.

The French and Indian wars ended in 1763. The long, trying wars had cost a great deal of money, and the British looked for ways to help pay for the war. One way was to make the American colonists pay more taxes to the British government. These new taxes would not only bring money into Britain, they would also remind the colonists that the British still controlled the colonies.

The taxes made many New Yorkers angry. Why should the people of New York, many of whom were not even British, have to pay the cost of Britain's wars? In 1765 people from 9 of the 13 British colonies agreed not to buy any British goods—to **boycott** them—until the government canceled the taxes.

The British did take back most of the new taxes, and some New Yorkers were satisfied that the boycott of British goods had succeeded. Some of these New Yorkers were **loyalists**, people who supported the British government. But other New Yorkers, and many people throughout the colonies, wanted to end British control forever. They decided to fight for independence.

Fort Ticonderoga was an important military base during the American War of Independence.

In 1775 colonial forces, calling themselves the Continental Army, entered the American War of Independence against the British. The following year, representatives from all 13 British colonies signed a statement, the Declaration of Independence. It stated that the colonies were free from British rule. The Declaration of Independence didn't end the war, however.

The British army captured Long Island and New York City in 1776. They occupied the area throughout the War of Independence. But the colonists fought hard. Even with the help of Iroquois, Montauk, and other Indian soldiers, the British could not take over all of New York. The first major colonial victory occurred at the Battle of Saratoga, in northeastern New York, in 1777.

The British defeated the colonists in the Battle of Long Island before taking over New York City.

With help from the French, and the many Indians who supported the French, the colonists eventually won the war. The British surrendered in 1781, and the colonists formed a new country—the United States of America. The two sides had fought many battles on New York soil, and many New Yorkers—colonists and Indians—had died.

During the war, American troops had destroyed many Iroquois villages, and some Iroquois who had fought with the British fled to Canada. After the war, the U.S. government forced the Iroquois who remained in New York to sell their land and move to **reservations**, small parcels of land reserved for Indians.

Control of New York now belonged to the former colonists. In 1788 they joined the new nation as its 11th state. They then turned to developing their state. The government gradually sold the land that it had taken from the Iroquois. People who had fought in the war were among the first white people to buy this newly available land. They established towns and farmed the fertile soil.

The War of 1812

Only 31 years after the War of Independence ended, New York was again a battleground in a fight against the British—the War of 1812. After the War of Independence, many British sailors left the British navy and went to work on U.S. ships. The British began stopping ships at sea and forcing any British-born sailors on board to return to the British navy.

To get the British to stop stealing sailors from U.S. ships, the United States refused to buy anything from Britain. When the British continued to steal sailors, the U.S. Congress declared war on Britain.

Many British troops were stationed in Canada, so towns near New York's Canadian border became major military bases for U.S. troops. New York contributed large numbers of ships and troops to the U.S. cause. The fighting ended in 1814 with the signing of the Treaty of Ghent.

In the early 1800s, Governor DeWitt Clinton persuaded the state government to build a canal to connect Lake Erie with the Hudson River. The Erie Canal, completed in 1825, made it easy to ship goods such as lumber, leather, and flour from the Midwest and western New York to the port at New York City. There the products were sent overseas to be sold. Banks were opened in New York City to manage the money that buyers and sellers made.

With land and jobs available all over the state, New York's popula-

New Yorkers could not agree on the official design for their flag until 1901. The flag features two women, Liberty *(left)* and Justice *(right),* and the state motto, *Excelsior,* meaning "Ever Upward."

The Erie Canal was opened in 1825 and helped make New York an important center of manufacturing and business.

tion grew and grew, especially in the cities. People came from other parts of the United States. **Immigrants,** people from other countries, moved to New York. Soon New York had more citizens than any state in the country.

The large population provided many workers for New York's factories, which produced a wide variety of goods, including flour, lumber, textiles (cloth), and leather goods. As farms and factories churned out more products and made more money, and as more banks and financial companies were opened to manage that money, New York became the country's center of trade, finance, and manufacturing.

33

In the 1860s during the Civil War, New York joined the Northern side, which fought to end slavery. Black people in New York didn't have the same rights as white people, but slavery had been outlawed in New York since 1827. Many New Yorkers were against slavery, and the state helped the North defeat the South by sending more men to fight than any other state.

As New York's population continued to grow throughout the 1800s, it became more and more varied. Immigrants were arriving in greater numbers and from more places than ever before. Some people called New York a **melting pot**, because it contained so many different "ingredients," or types of people.

Not all New Yorkers were opposed to slavery, and many were unwilling to go to war to end it. In July 1863, people protested against the Civil War by rioting in New York City's streets and burning buildings, including the homes of many black people.

First from Ireland, then from Italy, Poland, Germany, and elsewhere in Europe, hundreds of thousands of immigrants poured into the state. Even most immigrants who settled in other parts of the United States came through New York first. Government officials checked in new arrivals to the country at Ellis Island, an immigration station in New York Harbor.

Since it was built in 1885, the Statue of Liberty in New York Harbor has greeted immigrants with the hope of a better life in their new homeland, the United States of America.

Little Italy is one of many ethnic neighborhoods that sprang up in New York City during the early 1900s.

By 1900 one out of every three New Yorkers had been born in a foreign country. The newcomers often found jobs in the state's many factories, making different types of goods ranging from sewing machines to magazines, from cameras to clothes.

New York City's stock exchange was the center of the country's financial activity. There, people bought and sold **stocks,** or shares in the ownership of the nation's businesses. But in 1929, the prices of shares on the stock exchange crashed, or fell drastically. The stocks became nearly worthless, and stockholders lost huge amounts of money.

The stock market crash led to a period known as the Great Depression. When stock owners lost so much money, many businesses shut down. Stores closed down because people didn't want to spend the little money they had. Thousands of New Yorkers, like others across the land, lost jobs and had little money for food, clothing, and other needs.

Franklin D. Roosevelt, New York's governor, believed that the government should help its needy citizens. He created programs to provide food and medical care for poor families and to create jobs for people who were out of work.

In 1932 Roosevelt was elected president—the fifth U.S. president from New York. As president, he developed more programs, known as the New Deal, to help people who were suffering because of the Great Depression. Through the New Deal, Roosevelt helped lead his home state, and the country, out of the Great Depression. World War II further boosted the economy in the early 1940s. New York's factories bustled to prepare equipment for the troops overseas.

Many people who could not find work during the Great Depression worried about their futures.

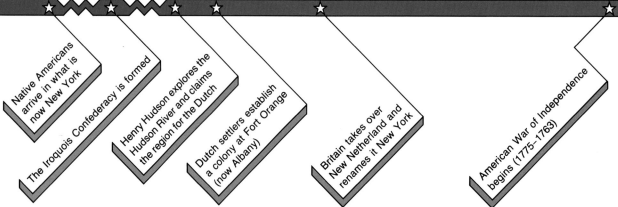

12,000 B.C.　A.D.1400　1609　1624　1663　1775

Native Americans arrive in what is now New York

The Iroquois Confederacy is formed

Henry Hudson explores the Hudson River and claims the region for the Dutch

Dutch settlers establish a colony at Fort Orange (now Albany)

Britain takes over New Netherland and renames it New York

American War of Independence begins (1775–1763)

By the late 1940s, New York had returned to its position as the country's leader in finance and manufacturing. A decade later, some industries began leaving New York for states with cheaper property and lower taxes, taking thousands of jobs with them. But most companies stayed, and New York is still one of the world's major business, finance, and manufacturing centers.

In recent years, New Yorkers have faced hard times. Poverty, crime, and homelessness are widespread in New York's cities, and the state's many races and ethnic groups do not always get along with each other. But most New Yorkers still find their state an exciting place to live, work, and play.

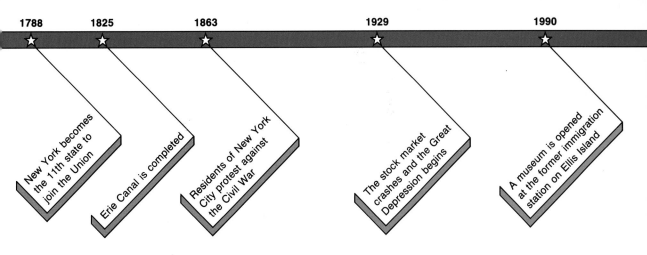

1788 New York becomes the 11th state to join the Union

1825 Erie Canal is completed

1863 Residents of New York City protest against the Civil War

1929 The stock market crashes and the Great Depression begins

1990 A museum is opened at the former immigration station on Ellis Island

The immigration station at Ellis Island in New York City was made into a museum in 1991.

41

The cities of Kingston, Poughkeepsie, and New York City were each New York's capital at one time. Albany didn't become the state capital until 1797. The capitol *(above)* was built in 1879.

Living and Working in New York

For almost as long as people have lived there, New York has had a varied population. Long before the Duke of York gave the area his name, numerous Native American tribes, each speaking a different language and following a different way of life, made their homes there. The millions of people—almost 18 million—who now live in New York have their origins in countries all over the world.

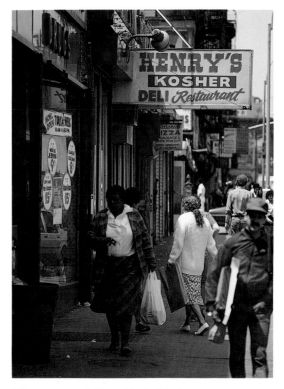

Like many of New York City's neighborhoods, the Lower East Side has a wide variety of people, stores, and restaurants.

Immigrants are still coming to New York in large numbers. Nowadays, over 10 percent of New Yorkers were born in foreign countries. Many of the newest immigrants come from Latin America and Asia, but the largest number of New Yorkers born outside the United States come from Italy.

New York also has more than two million African American residents, more than any other state in the country. More Jewish people live in New York than in any other state. Hispanics make up about 9 percent of the state's population. Over 38,000 Native Americans call New York home.

Most New Yorkers live in cities. New York City is the largest city in the country, with over eight million people, and nearly half of all New Yorkers live in the New York City area. Most other residents live in or near the state's other large cities, which include Buffalo, Rochester, and Syracuse. Only about 15 percent of New Yorkers live in small villages or other **rural** areas.

Even in New York's big cities, it's possible to find a quiet spot, such as New York City's Central Park.

People often come to New York from other states and countries to join family members who are already living there. But they also come because New York continues to be the business and cultural capital of the country and one of the most exciting places to live in the world.

The people who have moved to New York over the years have brought elements of their backgrounds to the state, creating a unique mix of cultures. As a result, New York can claim many of the greatest, and most varied, artistic opportunities in the country.

New York City's theaters are so famous that Broadway, the street that houses many of the theaters, has come to mean "theater." The city boasts dozens of museums and galleries, including the Metropolitan Museum of Art, the country's largest art museum.

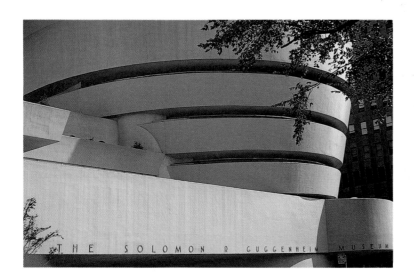

The Guggenheim Museum, in New York City, is famous for its unusual shape and its fine collection of modern art.

Opera singers perform at New York City's Metropolitan Opera House.

People who enjoy dance can watch a wide variety in New York City, from the traditional American Ballet Theatre to the modern Alvin Ailey Dance Company. For music lovers, there are concert halls such as the Metropolitan Opera House and Avery Fisher Hall, and nightclubs offering nearly every type of music imaginable.

Visitors have fun learning about cameras at Rochester's International Museum of Photography.

Elsewhere in the state, more cultural opportunities are available. Several cities, including Buffalo and Albany, have their own orchestras. Museums around the state include the International Museum of Photography in Rochester, the Corning Glass Center in Corning, and the National Baseball Hall of Fame in Cooperstown.

New Yorkers who like sports are lucky. Their state has two professional baseball teams, the New York Yankees and the New York Mets. Sports fans can also follow football's Buffalo Bills, New York Jets, and New York Giants. Three hockey teams, the New York Rangers, the New York Islanders, and the Buffalo Sabres, play in the state. Basketball fans can root for the New York Knicks.

When they're not watching one of the state's sports teams, some New Yorkers enjoy fishing, boating, and swimming at the state's ocean beaches or at its lakes. Many New Yorkers hike in the summer or ski in the winter.

48

Many New Yorkers enjoy winter sports such as sledding.

Baseball's New York Yankees are one of the state's many professional sports teams.

49

The Wall Street area, at the southern tip of Manhattan Island, is home to many of the nation's major financial companies.

On any weekday morning in any of New York's cities, thousands of people crowd the streets as they rush off to work. What do all those people, and the millions of other working New Yorkers, do for a living? About 65 percent of them work in jobs that provide services to people.

The best known service industry in New York is finance and banking. New York City is home to the New York Stock Exchange and to many other financial companies. Many New Yorkers work in other service jobs such as advertising, real estate (the buying and selling of property), and insurance (which protects people and their possessions).

Workers in New York's cities make a wide variety of goods, from books to clothing, from cameras to computers. In fact, manufacturing provides about 13 percent of the money made in New York every year. New York is the country's second biggest producer of manufactured goods. Only California makes more goods each year.

Some of the state's main manufacturing cities include Rochester, famous for photographic equipment, and Buffalo, where mill workers grind more flour than in any other city in the world. In Syracuse, electrical equipment and automobile parts are made. New York City's workers make more books, magazines, and other printed materials than workers in any other city in the nation.

Huge containers called elevators hold grain near a shipping port in Buffalo.

Apples are one of New York's most important farm products.

Farming is important to New York's economy, although not as important as it was in the mid-1800s, when wheat from New York was sold all over the country and in Europe. Milk is the state's leading agricultural product, but beef cattle, hay, corn, and fruit are widely produced too. In fact, New York produces more grapes than any state except California and more apples than any state but Washington.

Mining is not a major industry in New York. But New York's land yields many different mineral products. These include limestone, salt, natural gas, garnet, lead, and silver, which bring over a million dollars into the state each year.

The breathtaking sight of Niagara Falls attracts countless tourists every year.

Tourism is vital to New York's economy. New York City's sights, such as the Statue of Liberty and the Empire State Building, are famous worldwide. Many newlyweds spend their honeymoons at Niagara Falls in western New York. Other tourists admire the scenery of the Finger Lakes or the Adirondack Mountains. With its beauty, excitement, and variety, New York has something for all to enjoy.

Protecting the Environment

Whether they like exciting cities or beautiful countryside, people find many reasons to live in New York, and that's why so many live there. But every day, all those people produce garbage—at work or at school, at home, and elsewhere.

In fact, each New Yorker makes almost 7 pounds (3.2 kilograms) of garbage, or solid waste, a day. With nearly 18 million people in the state, that amounts to a lot of garbage. Since most of the state's land is used by people, New Yorkers have a hard time finding enough places to put all that waste.

Garbage is a big problem in New York, whether it's overflowing from a trash can on a city street *(left)* or scattered at the side of a country road *(above)*.

New Yorkers send most of their solid waste to **landfills,** areas of land where garbage is buried, and they've done so for many years. Recently, though, some of New York's landfills have begun to run out of room. Others have had to be closed because they were polluting the state's **groundwater,** the water supply below the earth's surface.

Landfills pollute groundwater when rotting garbage mixes with rainwater to create a liquid called **leachate.** Leachate is full of mate-

Fresh Kills, on Staten Island, is one of many overcrowded landfills in New York.

rials that pollute. The state government could choose to build new landfills, safe ones that won't leak. But that would be expensive, and New York has very little room to build new landfills.

New Yorkers could also ship their garbage to landfills in other states. But shipping garbage is expensive, especially since landfills in states close to New York are overcrowded too, and waste would have to be sent a long distance.

And few states are willing to take New York's garbage. Many New Yorkers discovered this in 1987, when the garbage barge *Mobro,* crammed with more than 3,000 tons of solid waste, left New York Harbor in search of a place to deposit its cargo.

Workers unload garbage at a New York landfill.

A barge loaded with garbage prepares for its journey.

The garbage came from the town of Islip, New York, but Islip's landfill was already full. After sailing for two months without finding any state willing to take the garbage, the barge returned to New York.

The *Mobro's* garbage was eventually burned. Burning is not usu-ally a good way to dispose of waste, however, because the smoke pollutes the air. In addition, plastics and other materials can pro-duce dangerous chemicals when they are burned. But if landfills are full and people don't want to burn waste, what can New Yorkers do with their garbage?

One way to deal with some of it is to **recycle**. Recycling is collecting and processing garbage for reuse. New York law requires people to separate recyclable garbage, such as newspapers and glass, from nonrecyclable items. New Yorkers have to pay a deposit when they buy drinks in cans and bottles. They get their money back if they return the empty can or bottle to the store for recycling.

New Yorkers are required to separate recyclable garbage from nonrecyclable.

Recycling is better than burning garbage or storing it in landfills, but many New Yorkers feel that it's important to concentrate on finding ways to produce less garbage in the first place.

New Yorkers can find many ways to do this. They can avoid buying **disposable** products—that is, items that are thrown away after they're used once. Simply reusing things—writing on both sides of a sheet of paper, sharing a magazine with friends instead of each person buying a copy, or cleaning out an empty jar to use for storage—can also cut down the amount of garbage produced.

New York's solid waste problem is not going to disappear, but it is getting better. About 15 percent of New York's garbage is now recycled, and that amount continues to increase. If everyone in New York tries to make less garbage, the state will be a cleaner, more pleasant place for the millions of people who live there.

By bringing recyclables to a recycling center, these New Yorkers are helping to solve the garbage problem in their state.

New York's Famous People

SOJOURNER TRUTH

ACTIVISTS & LEADERS

Deganawida (1550?–1600?), a Huron Indian, teamed up with Iroquois leader Hiawatha to develop the Great Peace, an agreement that led to peace among the Iroquois tribes. Deganawida lived most of his life in what is now western New York.

Fiorello LaGuardia (1882–1947) was the mayor of New York City from 1934 to 1945. He made many changes in the city, including creating and improving parks. The LaGuardia Airport in Queens County, New York, is named for him.

Sojourner Truth (1797–1883) was named Isabelle when she was born into slavery in Ulster County, New York. After being freed in 1828, she took the name Sojourner Truth and became known as a great speechmaker. She spoke out against slavery and for women's rights.

NORMAN ROCKWELL ▶

▲ GRANDMA MOSES

ARTISTS

Grandma Moses (1860–1961) (Anna Mary Robertson) didn't take up painting until she was 76 years old. Although she never took an art lesson, she gained fame painting simple pictures of country life. She was born in Greenwich, New York.

Norman Rockwell (1894–1978) is one of the best-loved artists in the United States. Many of his paintings show humorous scenes from everyday life. Rockwell was born in New York City.

ATHLETES

Lou Gehrig (1903–1941), born in New York City, was one of the greatest baseball players in history. He was first baseman for the New York Yankees for 14 years. In 1939 he was elected to the National Baseball Hall of Fame. Gehrig died of a muscular disease now referred to as Lou Gehrig's disease.

Michael Jordan (born 1963) signed on as a guard and forward for the Chicago Bulls basketball team in 1983, but he was born in Brooklyn, New York. Crowds come to his games to cheer his dunk shots and other skillful moves. He has played on the U.S. Olympic team, and the National Basketball Association has twice named him its most valuable player.

◄ **LOU GEHRIG**

◄ **JOHN D. ROCKEFELLER**

MICHAEL JORDAN ►

BUSINESS LEADERS

John D. Rockefeller (1839–1937) from Richford, New York, made his fortune in the oil business. He helped form the Standard Oil Company in 1870. Rockefeller gave away more than $500 million to help other people and organizations.

Donald Trump (born 1946) was born in New York City. During the 1980s, he built many large real estate complexes in Manhattan. He also built casinos in Atlantic City, New Jersey.

DONALD TRUMP ►

63

ENTERTAINERS

Lucille Ball (1911–1989) played the funny homemaker Lucy Ricardo in the popular 1950s television show "I Love Lucy." She was born in Jamestown, New York, and began her career as a dancer and actress in New York City.

Irving Berlin (1888–1989), a self-taught musician, composed many popular songs. His most famous are "God Bless America" and "White Christmas." Berlin moved to New York City when he was a young boy.

Leonard Bernstein (1918–1990) was a famous American composer and conductor. He composed many musicals, including "West Side Story." He was also the first American to become the musical director of the New York Philharmonic Orchestra.

▲ LUCILLE BALL

Tom Cruise (born 1962) comes from Syracuse, New York. He has starred in several major films, including *Risky Business, Top Gun, Rain Man,* and *Born on the Fourth of July.*

TOM CRUISE ▶

▲ WOODY ALLEN

FILMMAKERS

Woody Allen (born 1935), a film director and writer, frequently stars in his own movies. Most of his films are set in his beloved hometown of New York City. His movie *Annie Hall,* a comedy, won four Academy Awards. Other films include *Hannah and Her Sisters* and *Radio Days.*

Spike Lee (born 1957) grew up in Brooklyn, New York. He has directed several movies, including *She's Gotta Have It* and *Do the Right Thing.* He is known for his fast-paced, colorful movies that explore race relations.

SPIKE LEE ▶

George Eastman (1854–1932) started the Eastman Kodak Company in Rochester, New York, in 1880. The company quickly became one of the largest producers of photographic equipment in the world. Eastman also invented a lightweight, low-cost camera called the Kodak, which helped make photography a popular hobby for many Americans.

J. Robert Oppenheimer (1904–1967), known as the Father of the Atom Bomb, was director of the laboratory in Los Alamos, New Mexico, where the first atomic bomb was made in the 1940s. He later supported arms control and opposed the development of the hydrogen bomb, a very powerful type of atomic bomb, because of the huge risks it posed.

▲ GEORGE EASTMAN

◀ WALT WHITMAN

MADELEINE ▶ L'ENGLE

WRITERS

Madeleine L'Engle (born 1918) won the Newbery Medal in 1963 for her children's book *A Wrinkle in Time*. She was born in New York City.

Ezra Jack Keats (1916–1983) was an author and illustrator of children's books. Keats came from New York City and is known for his illustrations containing collages. He won the Caldecott Medal for *The Snowy Day* in 1963.

Walt Whitman (1819–1892) was born in West Hills on Long Island, New York, and grew up in Brooklyn. A poet, Whitman's most famous book is *Leaves of Grass*. He praised the United States and democracy in his poems.

65

Facts-at-a-Glance

Nickname: The Empire State
Song: "I Love New York"
Motto: *Excelsior* (Ever Upward)
Tree: sugar maple
Flower: rose
Bird: bluebird
Animal: beaver

Population: 17,990,455*
Rank in population, nationwide: 2nd
Area: 54,475 sq mi (141,090 sq km)
Rank in area, nationwide: 27th
Date and ranking of statehood:
  July 26, 1788, the 11th state
Capital: Albany
Major cities (and populations*):
  New York (7,322,564), Buffalo (328,123),
  Rochester (231,636), Yonkers (188,082),
  Syracuse (163,860), Albany (101,082)
U.S. senators: 2
U.S. representatives: 31
Electoral votes: 33

*1990 census

Places to visit: Niagara Falls in Niagara Falls, Empire State Building in New York City, National Baseball Hall of Fame in Cooperstown, Corning Glass Center in Corning, American Museum of Natural History in New York City

Annual Events: Ice Castle Extravaganza at Chautauqua Lake (Feb.), St. Patrick's Day Parade in New York City (March), Adirondack Hot Air Balloon Festival in Glens Falls (Sept.), Thanksgiving Day Parade in New York City (Nov.), Festival of Lights in Niagara Falls (Nov.–Jan.)

Natural resources: fertile soil, limestone, salt, sand and gravel, natural gas, emery, forests, water, petroleum

Agricultural products: milk, beef and dairy cattle, eggs, poultry, hogs, sheep, cabbages, potatoes, snap beans, sweet corn, apples, grapes, maple syrup

Manufactured goods: printed materials, photographic film, cameras, dental equipment, electrical equipment, machinery, chemicals, clothing

ENDANGERED AND THREATENED SPECIES
Mammals—sperm whale, right whale, gray wolf, cougar, eastern woodrat, Indiana bat
Birds—golden eagle, bald eagle, peregrine falcon, least tern, loggerhead shrike, eskimo curlew
Reptiles—leatherback sea turtle, Atlantic Ridley sea turtle, Massasauga rattlesnake
Fish—shortnose sturgeon, longjaw cisco, round whitefish, eastern sand darter, blue pike
Plants—green spleenwort, moonwort, sandplain gerardia, Nantucket Juneberry, bleedingheart, curly grass, giant pinedrops

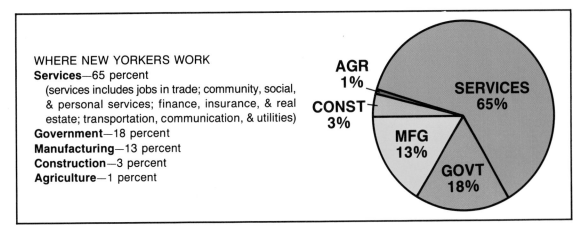

WHERE NEW YORKERS WORK
Services—65 percent
   (services includes jobs in trade; community, social, & personal services; finance, insurance, & real estate; transportation, communication, & utilities)
Government—18 percent
Manufacturing—13 percent
Construction—3 percent
Agriculture—1 percent

AGR 1%
CONST 3%
MFG 13%
GOVT 18%
SERVICES 65%

PRONUNCIATION GUIDE

Adirondack (ad-uh-RAHN-dak)

Algonquian (al-GAHN-kwee-uhn)

Appalachian (ap-uh-LAY-chuhn)

Iroquois (IHR-uh-kwoy)

Mahican (muh-HEE-kuhn)

Montauk (MAHN-TAWK)

Oneida (oh-NYD-uh)

Seneca (SEHN-ih-kuh)

Stuyvesant, Peter
(STY-vuh-suhnt, PEET-ur)

Syracuse (SIHR-uh-kyoos)

Tuscarora (tuhs-kuh-ROHR-uh)

Wappinger (WAH-pihn-jur)

Glossary

borough One of the five counties of New York City. The five boroughs are the Bronx, Brooklyn, Manhattan, Queens, and Staten Island.

boycott To refuse to buy, sell, or use something or to have any dealings with someone.

colony A territory ruled by a country some distance away.

glacier A large body of ice and snow that moves slowly over land.

Great Lakes A chain of five lakes in Canada and the northern United States. They are Lakes Superior, Michigan, Huron, Erie, and Ontario.

groundwater Water that lies beneath the earth's surface. The water comes from rain and snow that seep through soil into the cracks and other openings in rocks. Groundwater supplies wells and springs.

immigrant A person who moves into a foreign country and settles there.

landfill A place specially prepared for burying solid waste.

leachate Liquid formed by the decomposition of waste in a landfill.

loyalist A person who supports the government during a revolt.

melting pot A place where people of many different nationalities and races live and blend.

precipitation Forms of moisture such as rain, snow, and hail.

reservation Public land set aside by the government to be used by Native Americans.

rural Having to do with the countryside or farming.

stock A share in the ownership of a business. Stocks are bought and sold at stock exchanges.

Index ▰▰▰▰▰▰

Acknowledgments:

James Mejuto Photo, pp. 2–3, 49 (left), 54, 55 (both), 59, 61; Maryland Cartographics, pp. 2, 11; Jack Lindstrom, pp. 6, 7; Tony LaGruth, pp. 8 (left), 40, 45; © Gerry Lemmo, pp. 8–9, 10, 14, 16 (right), 28; New York State Department of Economic Development, pp. 13, 42, 50, 52; Hudson River Valley Association, pp. 15, 22; Betty Groskin, pp. 16 (left), 57; Monica V. Brown, Photographic Artist, pp. 17, 46; New-York Historical Society, New York City, pp. 18, 20, 23, 31, 33; Picture Collection, The Branch Libraries, The New York Public Library, p. 19; Library of Congress, pp. 24, 34–35, 37, 39, 62 (middle right), 65 (top right); New York State Historical Association, Cooperstown, p. 25; The Brooklyn Historical Society, p. 29; Statue of Liberty National Monument, p. 36; © Shmuel Thaler, p. 43; Metropolitan Opera/Winnie Klotz, p. 47; International Museum of Photography at George Eastman House, Education Department, p. 48; Yankees Magazine, p. 49 (right); James Blank/Root Resources, pp. 51, 53; © Arthur Morris/Visuals Unlimited, p. 56; NYC Department of Sanitation, p. 58; Minneapolis Public Library and Information Center, p. 62 (top); National Archives, p. 62 (bottom); The Bettman Archive, p. 63 (bottom right); Chicago Bulls, p. 63 (middle left); New York Yankees, p. 63 (top right); Hollywood Book and Poster, Inc., p. 64 (top right, middle left, bottom right); Independent Picture Service, pp. 63 (bottom left), 64 (middle left); The Pennsylvania Academy of the Fine Arts, p. 65 (bottom left), © James Phillips 1989, p. 65 (bottom right); Jean Matheny, p. 66; Albany County Convention and Visitors Bureau, p. 69; Thomas P. Benincas Jr., p. 71.